COLIN

Based on *The Railway Series* by the Rev. W. Awdry

Illustrations by
Robin Davies and *Jerry Smith*

EGMONT

EGMONT

We bring stories to life

First published in Great Britain 2009
by Egmont UK Limited
239 Kensington High Street, London W8 6SA

Thomas the Tank Engine & Friends™

CREATED BY BRITT ALLCROFT

Based on the Railway Series by the Reverend W Awdry
© 2009 Gullane (Thomas) LLC. A HIT Entertainment company.
Thomas the Tank Engine & Friends and Thomas & Friends are trademarks of Gullane (Thomas) Limited.
Thomas the Tank Engine & Friends and Design is Reg. U.S. Pat. & Tm. Off.

HiT entertainment

ISBN 978 1 4052 4421 3
1 3 5 7 9 10 8 6 4 2
Printed in Italy

FSC

Mixed Sources
Product group from well-managed
forests and other controlled sources

Cert no. TT-COC-002332
www.fsc.org
© 1996 Forest Stewardship Council

Egmont is passionate about helping to preserve the world's remaining ancient forests.
We only use paper from legal and sustainable forest sources.

This book is made from paper certified by the Forestry Stewardship Council (FSC),
an organisation dedicated to promoting responsible management of forest resources.
For more information on the FSC, please visit www.fsc.org. To learn more about
Egmont's sustainable paper policy, please visit www.egmont.co.uk/ethical

This is a story about Colin, a crane who works at the Wharf. While everyone gets ready for a party, Colin looks set to spend the night alone. But with good friends to help, he may just get some cheer after all!

It was a frosty afternoon on Sodor. Colin was hard at work at the Wharf.

Colin was a shiny green crane. He had a long arm that was Really Useful for carrying things.

That evening, a party for the children of Sodor was being held in The Thin Controller's garden. His house was near the Engine Depot, so the engines could enjoy the party, too!

Colin's friend, Freddie, was very excited. "There will be presents and fireworks!" he said.

But Colin didn't look quite so excited.

Just then, The Thin Controller cycled into the Wharf. "All of these crates must be unloaded before I leave for the party tonight," he told Colin.

"You can count on me!" Colin replied.

"I must go now," said The Thin Controller. "I'll be back later for Freddie to take me to the party."

The Thin Controller rode away on his bicycle.

"It will be the best party ever!" Freddie peeped.

Colin still didn't look excited. He couldn't go to the party. He had to stay at the Wharf. He didn't have wheels like the engines.

"I've never been to a party," Colin sighed.

Freddie felt sorry for his friend. Then suddenly, he had an idea!

"If I move the party to the Wharf," Freddie thought, "Colin can have his first surprise party!"

Freddie steamed out of the Wharf to put his exciting plan into action!

Freddie's first job was to find The Thin Controller. On his way, he pulled up by Peter Sam and Rusty.

Peter Sam was pulling a flatbed filled with crates. The crates had lots of colourful lights and presents on top.

Rusty was pulling another flatbed. It was piled high with boxes of fireworks.

"We're taking the cargo to The Thin Controller's house," Rusty told Freddie, "for the party!"

"The party is now at the Wharf!" puffed Freddie. "I'll take your flatbeds back there. Will you tell the other engines?"

Peter Sam and Rusty were very surprised but they agreed to help.

By the time Freddie had chuffed back into the Wharf with the flatbeds, the snow had settled on the ground. "Please leave this cargo here until I come back!" he told Colin.

Colin was puzzled. "Doesn't The Thin Controller need the cargo for his party?" he thought.

Later that afternoon, Thomas brought The Thin Controller back to the Wharf. When he saw the presents, lights and fireworks, he was very cross.

"They should be at my house for the party!" The Thin Controller shouted. "Colin, load them on to the barge!"

Colin didn't want to get Freddie into trouble so he kept quiet. He carefully loaded all of the cargo on to the barge.

When he had finished, the barge set off down the canal towards The Thin Controller's house.

Freddie steamed all over Sodor. He couldn't find The Thin Controller anywhere. Snow was falling heavily and it was getting late. He still hadn't asked if he could move the party!

When Freddie finally spluttered back into the Wharf, he was very tired.

Colin was waiting for his friend. He told him all about The Thin Controller's visit. "He asked me to send the party cargo down the canal," Colin said. "So, it's all done!"

Colin was very pleased. But Freddie wasn't pleased at all!

The children would be arriving at The Thin Controller's house in half an hour. There was nothing for the party there. And there was nothing at the Wharf!

Freddie felt terrible. "Which way did the barge go?" he asked Colin.

Colin pointed his long crane arm down the canal. And Freddie steamed off to find the barge.

The Thin Controller was very cross when Freddie finally pulled up next to him.

"Where have you been, Freddie?" he snapped.

Freddie told him about his idea to move the party to the Wharf. "I'm so sorry, sir," he sniffed.

The Thin Controller was quiet for a few moments. "You should have asked me first," he sighed, "but you can have the party at the Wharf!"

Freddie let out a happy toot! He just hoped he could find the barge before it was too late.

By the time Freddie caught up with the barge carrying the party cargo, it was almost dark.

"Stop!" he called to the Barge Man. "Please turn the barge around and go back to Colin. The party is now at the Wharf!"

The Barge Man was very surprised but he quickly stopped the barge.

Then Freddie headed back to find Colin. It was time he told his friend what was going on!

When Freddie pulled into the Wharf, Colin had just finished his work for the day.

"Have I got a story to tell you!" puffed Freddie. He began to tell Colin all about his party plans.

Colin was surprised and delighted. "You moved the party for me?" he blushed. "Well, we'd better get to work!"

The friends quickly hatched a plan. Freddie steamed off to collect the children, while Colin waited for the barge to arrive with the cargo. He had some unloading to do!

Colin moved the cargo in record time.

When Freddie arrived with the children, everyone gasped. The Wharf was filled with presents and lights. Many of the engines were there, too!

Then suddenly, a loud bang echoed around the Wharf. One after another, colourful fireworks shot up into the night sky!

"Wow! Thank you so much, Freddie!" smiled Colin, happily. "I'll never forget my first party!"

The engines whistled and the children cheered. It was the best party ever!

Two Great Offers for Thomas Fans!

THOMAS & FRIENDS

In every Thomas Story Library book like this one, you will find a special token. Collect the tokens and claim exclusive Thomas goodies:

Offer 1

Collect 6 tokens and we'll send you a **poster** and a **bookmark** for only **£1.**
(to cover P&P)

offer 2

Collect 12 tokens and we'll send you a choo-choo-tastic book bag for only £2. (to cover P&P)

So go on, start your Thomas Story Library now!
Available to buy online at **www.egmont.co.uk**

Simply tape a £1 or £2 coin in the space above, and fill in the form overleaf.

The Thomas bag contains 7 specially designed pockets to hold Thomas Story Library books. Please note that the books featured in the picture above are not included in the offer.

Reply Card for Thomas Goodies!

1 Yes, please send me a **Thomas poster and bookmark.**
I have enclosed **6 tokens plus a £1 coin** to cover P&P. ☐

2 Yes, please send me a **Thomas book bag.**
I have enclosed **12 tokens plus £2** to cover P&P. ☐

Simply fill in your details below and send them to:
Thomas Offers, PO BOX 715, Horsham, RH12 5WG

Fan's Name: ....

Address: ....

....

.... Date of Birth: ....

Email: ....

Name of parent/guardian: ....

Signature of parent/guardian: ....